The Mystery of the Golden Stars

An adventure in the European Union

CHAPTER I

THE INTRUDER

The intruder had disabled the burglar alarm with ease. Moments later, he had cracked the pin code to the heavy basement door. Now the intruder stood just inside the large, dark room. He swept a brilliant beam of torch light across a vast number of priceless stolen works of art. The beam came to rest on a life-sized bust: carved from pure white marble, it was a statue of the head and shoulders of a proud, powerful-looking man with a long, thin nose and a cruel mouth. But the intruder wasn't interested in the statue itself. Instead, with two hands he lifted a circular object off the top of the bust. He put the artefact inside a small rucksack and carefully did up the zip, before leaving the basement room of treasures. As he slipped back outside into the bitter night, he immediately reached into his jacket for his phone and began to text.

Seconds later, in a bedroom hundreds of miles away, a mobile phone buzzed and twitched like an angry wasp. From under the covers, a girl reached out a floppy arm and fumbled for her phone. She peered sleepily at the message on screen. It was a text from a number she recognised immediately. She shot upright in bed, her mind jolted from its slumber. Hardly daring to believe her eyes, she smiled down at the words:

'The flea market, the day after tomorrow. Dad.'

CHAPTER 2

MUD AND MIST

Twenty-four hours later

The intruder understood that he was taking a huge risk. If there had been any passers-by, a man on his hands and knees in such a public place would have attracted a lot of attention. The intruder, his face streaked with soil, clawed urgently with his bare hands at the water-logged earth. All of a sudden, he stopped, sprang upright on his aching knees and surveyed his surroundings. His eyes were bright and keen with fear. Convinced that he was still alone, he bent over again and withdrew a small object from his rucksack. For a moment, he held the object carefully over the shallow hole in the soil. The sound of an approaching car pierced the rattle of the rain and snapped him out of his reverie. He flattened himself on the ground, barely daring to lift his head from the wet grass. A few seconds later, it was clear that the car had moved on.

Without a moment's pause, he forced the object deep into the hole and filled it with the surrounding mud. Moments later, he scuttled like a crab to another patch of earth and began to dig again. His work here had only just started.

Several hours later, with the storm passed, the spring sun was glowing milkily through the low mist. A handful of market traders were setting up their stalls in the Place du Jeu de Balle in the centre of Brussels. Within a couple of hours the flea market, one of the most popular open-air markets in Europe, would be heaving with locals, antique collectors, curious tourists and bargain hunters. But for now, the traders went about their business laying out their goods on tables and boxes around the cobbled square.

So it was that the intruder, dressed in mud-caked trousers and a jacket, slipped quietly into the square. Approaching the stall of a yawning bric-a-brac dealer, he stopped and pretended to tie his shoelace. With the dealer's back turned, he reached inside his rucksack for the final time that day and pulled out a tatty toy. He placed it quickly in a crate with some other items.

The intruder moved on down a side street. He felt a mixture of relief and satisfaction, yet his eyes betrayed a deep, gnawing fear. He considered how lucky he had been that there had been no passers-by that night. How lucky that there had been so few people at the flea market and that the mist had not yet lifted. Indeed, much of this was true, yet since dawn he had never really been alone.

CHAPTER 3

THE BEAR NECESSITIES

It was 9 o'clock and Josh and Ricki were finding it hard to know where to start. In front of them, the busy flea market throbbed with visitors peering at antiques and poking through boxes of junk.

Josh, wrapped up neatly against the cold, stood next to his friend. Ricki wore a thin fleece which was open at the front and slipping off his bony shoulders. His hands were stuffed deep inside his pockets and unruly curls of hair sprang out around the edges of his woolly hat.

'Look at all this beautiful junk!' said Ricki excitedly. 'We're bound to find something brilliant today in all this stuff. Let's start with those crates of books over there. Come on!'

They stepped forward into the crowds. Josh felt a rush of excitement as he began to inspect some of the items on sale more closely. Here they both were in Brussels, the capital city of Belgium. It was also the home of one of their heroes — Hergé, the author of Tintin. Both boys had read every Tintin comic book many times over. Now they felt just like their favourite boy detective searching the market for something exciting: an old figurine, a T-shirt, some playing cards, a signed copy of a book, anything to add to their Tintin collections at home.

A couple of hours later, the two boys were feeling disappointed. They had turned up nothing, except a battered Tintin lunch box, which Ricki already had. The crowds were drifting away and some of the traders were beginning to dismantle their stalls in time for an early lunch.

'Stupid flea market, what a waste of time,' muttered Ricki. 'I want to smash something.'

Josh was used to his friend's short temper and tried to calm him down before things got out of hand.

'Ricki, listen to me. Let's get a hot chocolate and make another plan.'

'No!' growled Ricki and spun around looking for something to punch or kick. The nearest crate went flying, the contents clattering across the cobbles.

'Oh là, attention!' exclaimed the market trader, turning to face the boys angrily.

'Pardon, monsieur, pardon,' Josh stepped in, expertly guiding his fuming friend to a safe distance and scrambling to pick up the scattered items. The trader stared at him suspiciously and watched as Josh replaced his wares into the crate. He raised his hand abruptly for Josh to stop and pointed at the crate.

'C'est cassé, l'ours est cassé,' he snarled.

'Pardon, monsieur, I don't understand,' Josh stuttered.

'Eenglish?'

Josh nodded.

'The bear,' the man continued pointing, 'the bear is broken. You have to pay for it.'

Josh looked down and saw a tatty soft toy bear. An eye was missing, the fur was wearing thin in places and now one arm was held on by a thread, the result of Ricki's furious kick.

'Oui, monsieur, how much? Combien?'

'Ten euros,' he replied.

Josh sighed and handed over a €10 note.

'Why, Ricki? Well? Why can't you just control yourself? Thanks to you, this is what we've got to show for our morning. A stupid bear!'

He thrust the toy inches from Ricki's face. Ricki glanced at it sheepishly and then, to Josh's surprise, began to examine it closely. Josh, still flushed with anger, watched Ricki's eyes open wider and his mouth form a broad smile.

'Look inside, Josh,' he said. Josh peered closer. Poking out from the tufts of stuffing he noticed the crinkled edge of an envelope.

'What on earth …' he heard himself saying, as Ricki began to rip clumsily at the remaining stitching.

Seconds later, the boys were staring in wonder at a small padded envelope. All of a sudden, they seemed frozen by the potential of the discovery. Slowly, Ricki eased his finger under the flap and began to break the seal. As the flap finally lifted free, a voice sounded close behind them.

'Mon ours, my bear, you have destroyed my bear!'

Spinning round, the boys found themselves face-to-face with their angry accuser, a dark-haired girl around their age. Josh and Ricki looked down at the discarded soft toy.

'We're sorry, we just bought it and, we didn't know …' garbled Ricki.

'You had no right, it's mine,' the girl continued. 'My dad sent me a text. He told me to come here. I think I saw him but it was misty and he disappeared. I've been looking for him all morning.'

Josh tried to make some sense of her story. Many questions bubbled up, but instead he blurted:

'Hi. I'm Josh. This is Ricki. What's your name?'

'Maddy,' she replied.

'Hi, Maddy, we're sorry about your bear but let me get this straight. Your dad took your bear and left it here in the market and texted you to come here too? Why would he do that?'

'I don't know, my dad does strange things sometimes. We live here in Brussels but I haven't seen him for a few days.'

Ricki was finding it hard to contain his growing excitement. What mystery had they discovered? Who was involved? Ricki liked the sound of Maddy's mysterious dad. He stared at the envelope clutched in his fingers.

'We found this,' he said, waving it excitedly at her. Maddy looked confused. 'It was inside your bear. We've just opened it, but maybe you should be the first one to see what's inside.'

He held the envelope out towards her. The boys watched as she unfolded a small pack of papers. She spread them out carefully on a nearby trader's table and the three of them pored over them eagerly. There were handwritten notes, scraps of paper with jumbled letters and numbers, fragments of pictures and photocopies of old letters.

'Have you seen any of these before, Maddy?' asked Josh.

'No, but it all belongs to my dad. I recognise his handwriting.'

'Well, kids,' said Ricki, beaming, 'it looks like we've got a mystery to solve. So, where do we start?'

Josh picked up the nearest item that he recognised: a map of Europe. He turned it over and they all stared at a short list of incomprehensible notes.

'The title says it's a map of something called the European Union. Perhaps these notes are clues to some places on the map, a bit like coordinates,' Josh mused. 'There seems to be a map key too, but it's not complete.'

'What's the European Union?' asked Ricki.

'I'm not sure but I think we should find out and complete the map,' said Josh.

'I know just the place,' added Maddy excitedly. 'It's called Mini-Europe. It's a giant model version of the whole continent. I bet we'll find some answers there.'

'You know what? I can use my smartphone to e-mail our friends at school for some help,' said Josh.

With that, they headed for the underground station, the sun now bright in the cloudless spring sky overhead.

To: class@myschool.sch.uk

From: joshphone@visitbrussels.eu

Subject: **First Clue – EU countries?**

Attachment: mapoftheeu.doc

We have found a map of Europe with a puzzling list on it.
We need your help finding out more about which countries
are members of the European Union and their capitals.
Maddy told us that the EU has expanded with new countries
joining regularly. There were six Member States at the start.
Now there are 28! First, we need you to colour the map
using different colours to show when each country joined.
A list of Member States and dates is included. Then see if
you can use your map to solve the puzzling list. We think it
might spell a special word.

Good luck!

Josh, Ricki and our new Belgian friend Maddy

CHAPTER 4

THE STAR CIPHER

Josh locked the screen on his smartphone and shoved it back into his jeans.

'Just as we thought,' he said, grinning. 'We were right about the first clue, but I'm glad the guys at school agree.'

'Mini-Europe was great at eye-level, but it's even better from up here,' enthused Ricki, whose nose was pressed against a large window.

The children were standing 100 metres above the ground in the upper sphere of the Atomium. Josh read from his visitor's guide:

'Built in 1958, the Atomium is a striking monument and key landmark on the Brussels skyline. It is constructed of nine interconnected steel spheres that form the shape of an iron crystal magnified 165 billion times.'

Standing a little way back from the window, Maddy stood, arms folded, staring south over the city. Her eyes were dark and sombre. Josh, who knew a thing or two about foul moods, approached gently.

'Maddy, are you OK?'

'I don't like heights,' she snapped. Josh nodded sympathetically, sensing that vertigo wasn't really the problem.

'Listen, we solved a clue. Where's that envelope? We'll solve the other puzzles together. We can do it and help you find your dad.'

'Let's have another look at the package of papers then,' said Josh smiling.

The children sifted through the papers for several minutes, but nothing presented itself as an easy clue.

'Your dad's cool, setting you puzzles like this,' said Ricki suddenly.

'Well, he loves solving puzzles,' Maddy explained quietly. 'Actually, what he really likes is designing puzzles, creating crosswords, drawing optical illusions, that sort of thing.'

The boys were listening intently. Josh asked, 'What's his job?'

'He goes away on business a lot. He was always secretive. He used to argue with my mum about it. A few months ago, she left us and my aunt looks after me now when he's away.

I went to meet him this morning but he disappeared again,' she said, a tremor of sadness in her voice.

'Look, how about this?' Josh said, holding up two sheets of paper joined at an edge. 'This top sheet looks like a flag that's been through a shredder. The sheet underneath seems to be a page of random letters.'

'No, it's not,' said Maddy eagerly. 'I recognise this type of puzzle. The bottom sheet isn't random at all. It's a cipher. You use it to decode a message.'

Ricki smiled broadly and slapped them both on the back.

'I've got it! It's a bit like the last puzzle. We need to complete the flag. See, there are some golden stars on it. Looking at the pattern, I bet some of them are missing. I reckon we'll find the letters we need on the cipher under the missing stars.'

'Brilliant, Ricki,' exclaimed Josh, impressed by his friend's theory. 'So, all we need to do is figure out where the missing stars go, right?'

Suddenly, a bright flash of reflected sunlight caught Josh's attention and instinctively he scanned the room for the source. The sunlight was reflecting off an odd-looking hand protruding from a neat, black suit sleeve. It was slender and delicate and

fashioned from some lustrous metal. Yet, Josh was unnerved by it. At first, the hand seemed immobile, stuck like a claw, the lean fingers and thumb held rigid. If he had blinked just then though, he would have missed it: like the strike of a snake, the golden claw flicked open and snapped shut again. A trickle of fear ran down Josh's spine. Another flare of golden light blinded him momentarily and when he'd blinked it away, the sinister hand and its owner had disappeared.

'There are loads of flags like this outside the European Commission building back in the city centre,' Maddy was explaining to Ricki. She turned to Josh, giving him a puzzled look.

'What's the matter? You look really spooked,' she said.

'Listen,' said Josh, 'I'm not sure we should stay here any longer. And I think we should be more careful with these papers. I don't know, maybe it's nothing, but it just struck me that we might not be the only ones looking for your dad.'

With that, they returned to the centre of Brussels.

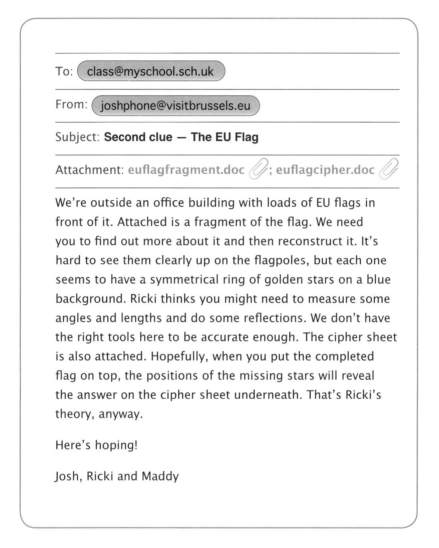

To: class@myschool.sch.uk

From: joshphone@visitbrussels.eu

Subject: **Second clue — The EU Flag**

Attachment: euflagfragment.doc ; euflagcipher.doc

We're outside an office building with loads of EU flags in front of it. Attached is a fragment of the flag. We need you to find out more about it and then reconstruct it. It's hard to see them clearly up on the flagpoles, but each one seems to have a symmetrical ring of golden stars on a blue background. Ricki thinks you might need to measure some angles and lengths and do some reflections. We don't have the right tools here to be accurate enough. The cipher sheet is also attached. Hopefully, when you put the completed flag on top, the positions of the missing stars will reveal the answer on the cipher sheet underneath. That's Ricki's theory, anyway.

Here's hoping!

Josh, Ricki and Maddy

CHAPTER 5

THE CURSED CROWN

'There are so many flags, but I can't see any of them properly. Where's the wind when you need it?'

Ricki was peering up at a row of limp flags on silver-coloured poles in front of a large office building. 'What's this place, anyway?'

'According to my guidebook, this is called the Berlaymont. It's the headquarters of the European Commission, which helps run the EU,' replied Josh. 'People from all over Europe work there and apparently they use 24 different languages.'

'Why not 28?' asked Ricki.

'Some countries like Germany and Austria speak the same language,' Josh went on.

'And these are all EU flags, right?' Ricki wanted to know.

'Hang on,' said Josh, 'I just got an e-mail … yes! The guys at school have solved it, look.'

Josh read aloud, 'The EU flag consists of 12 golden stars in a circle on a blue background. The stars symbolise harmony among the peoples of Europe. The number twelve is a symbol of perfection and the circle is a symbol of unity.'

'Yes, but what did the cipher reveal?' Maddy asked excitedly.

Josh scrolled down and pointed, 'Here. That's the next clue word.'

All three stood quietly for several seconds, staring disappointedly at the word, hoping some meaning would leap to mind.

'I don't get it,' said Ricki. 'It's all a bit random, isn't it? Anyone for a milkshake?'

A short time later, the children were sitting outside a cafe back in the centre of the city, the bright sun warming their backs. Ricki slurped noisily at the remains of his milkshake. Josh ignored him and said, 'We now have two clue words, 'Schengen' and 'Ted Heath', but what are they for? What are we supposed to be solving? Maddy?'

'Maybe the words … what if … ' Maddy began. 'I don't know, Josh. I just hope that they will lead us to my dad.'

Ricki stood up without a word, his eyes fixed on a newspaper kiosk across the street. Maddy and Josh watched as he dodged a couple of beeping scooters and headed towards the kiosk, where he whisked the top newspaper off a pile, paid the kiosk owner with a cheerful 'merci' and sauntered back across the street.

'Really?' Maddy blurted. 'This is how you help? By relaxing with a newspaper?'

Ricki unfolded the newspaper and threw it down on the cafe table dramatically.

'Ta-daaa!' he beamed triumphantly.

The two others stared down at the headline on the front page which read: 'CURSED CROWN STOLEN!!!'

'Well?' Josh looked up at his friend. Seeing that Ricki was revelling in his own cleverness and had no intention of explaining, Josh read the article instead:

The News

CURSED CROWN STOLEN!!!

Police discover break-in at mysterious private villa

Priceless gold crown may still exist

The *Corona Crassus*, known as the cursed crown, has not been seen for many years. However, evidence that it still exists emerged yesterday following a break-in at a remote private villa in Italy. A local police patrol discovered an underground safe room full of stolen artworks and jewellery. Strangely, forensics revealed that only one item seemed to be missing. Sources close to the police admitted sensationally that the item may be the fabled cursed crown.

The *Corona Crassus* is a single headband of solid gold surrounded by a ring of twelve five-pointed stars. It belonged to a powerful, ruthless Roman politician called Marcus Licinius Crassus, one of the wealthiest people in ancient history. The secretive owners of the villa were not home at the time and the police are trying to locate them. The police are also offering a reward for any information that helps in the recovery of the crown.

Police investigate links to organised crime gangs involved in trade of ancient artifacts

The details from the article and the events of the day swirled round Josh's head. Could there be a connection? Twelve golden stars, a missing crown, a Roman called Crassus, a teddy bear stuffed with clues and three kids in Belgium. What were they involved in? The fog of facts and events evaporated in his mind as he rejected the whole idea as a coincidence.

'I know what you're thinking, Ricki,' Josh said, 'but that's crazy. We're looking for Maddy's dad, that's all. You don't seriously believe this is some sort of treasure hunt?'

Ricki explained his theory confidently, 'Think about it. A few days ago, a crown covered in golden stars was stolen. This morning, Maddy's dad hides a bunch of clues, including one about a flag with — you guessed it — twelve golden stars on it!'

Josh turned to Maddy for support. 'I know you said your dad was mixed up in some secretive stuff, but cursed crowns belonging to dead Romans? Come off it.'

'I don't know,' she replied slowly, still reading the article carefully. 'I think Ricki might be right.'

'OK, you win. We're looking for your dad *and* a cursed golden crown,' Josh sighed and slumped back in his chair. 'So, come on, let's have a look at the next clue.'

Maddy hurriedly pulled the envelope of clues out of her bag and spread several photos out across the cafe table.

'I thought these looked interesting. This seems to be a photo from the Second World War. And look at this one of lots of men in a posh room. One of the men is circled.'

There was also a handwritten note on the photo, which Josh read aloud: "Right-hand man". Hmm, I wonder who he was.'

Ricki pointed to a scrap of paper. 'This seems to be some sort of diary entry,' he remarked.

'Right, I'll take pictures of all these and e-mail them to our school to see if they can help again,' said Josh.

'There's a museum near here that contains lots of historical letters and documents from the war. We should show the photos to somebody there,' added Maddy.

Thirty seconds after the children had left, another customer inside the cafe beckoned to the waiter.

'The bill,' the voice was deep and forceful.

'Oui, madame,' replied the waiter. The customer lifted a tall glass of water to her thin, colourless lips and drank it down silently. The waiter bustled back towards her with the bill. The woman turned her face up towards his. Holding his gaze, she picked up her glass again, holding it lightly between the thumb and fingers of a hand made of gold. Without warning, the fingers snapped shut effortlessly. The sound of shattering glass rang out. Although she neither paid nor apologised, the waiter was relieved to see her stalk out of the cafe heading in the same direction as the three children.

To: class@myschool.sch.uk

From: joshphone@visitbrussels.eu

Subject: **Third clue — Old photos**

Attachment: warphotos.doc 📎; diaryentry.doc 📎

Hi guys

We need your help again! Can you find out anything about these photos? We also need to identify a man who has been circled in one of the pictures. There's a diary entry about some event called the Schuman declaration too. What was that all about? Let us know if you find out the name of the mystery man in the photo.

Thanks!

Josh, Ricki and Maddy

CHAPTER 6

THE GOLDEN CLAW

'Just remind me, where did you say you got hold of these photos?' asked the woman gently from behind the museum desk. Sarah Van de Velde looked up over the top of her glasses to study the faces of the three children in front of her. As a curator at the Museum of Letters and Manuscripts, Sarah was used to dealing with rare and interesting documents, but her natural curiosity had been aroused by the arrival of these three strange children and their envelope of materials.

'We're doing a school history project and thought you might be able to help,' said Josh.

'We think we know who this man is,' said Maddy abruptly, pointing to the man circled in one of the photos, 'but could you tell us a bit more about him?' Sarah studied the images and diary entry and for a few minutes told the children what she knew about Jean Monnet, Robert Schuman and the declaration. The children listened intently as Sarah explained.

'Robert Schuman really is a celebrated figure in Europe. For example, there's a Schuman railway station, a Schuman metro and even a Schuman roundabout here in Brussels,' she explained. Engrossed in her stories, they all jumped when a deep voice interrupted her from behind them.

'There you are, children,' the voice purred. 'Has the nice lady helped you find the answer?'

A lean woman towered over them. A pair of flinty green eyes glared out from underneath black eyebrows smeared together across a prominent brow. Her nose was narrow and sharp, her jaw angular and a network of blood vessels criss-crossed her pale cheeks like thin blue scars.

'Thank you for your help, but we must all be going. Come on, children, we have a train to catch back to school,' she ordered.

The children didn't move an inch. Sarah saw a flash of fear pass across Josh's face. She looked up at the woman. There was something pitiless about her eyes, like a reptilian predator.

'And you are … ?' asked Sarah, her suspicions growing with every moment.

'Madame Crass. I am their teacher,' replied the woman, a hint of impatience entering her tone.

'Please may I see some ID, Madame Crass,' said Sarah, doing her best to hold the woman's stare.

'I've wasted enough time,' she said, her voice deeper and dangerous. 'Give me that envelope.'

'This woman's not our teacher, we don't know her, help us Sarah!' blurted Ricki.

Maddy was first to react, scooping up the photos and the envelope before ducking round the desk and sprinting off between a long aisle of tall display cases. Sarah, a look of deep shock and confusion on her face, recovered her composure and radioed the museum security guards and then immediately phoned the police. Crass set off in pursuit of Maddy, her face a mask of determination. Ricki bolted into a parallel aisle in the same direction as Maddy and Crass. Josh saw that Crass was about to catch up with Maddy and called out to warn her. Without breaking her stride, Maddy flung the envelope up and to her right. It tumbled over the top of the tall display case and landed in front of Ricki in the next aisle. Crass glared at Maddy and bounded powerfully back along the aisle and disappeared around the corner. Within seconds she had cornered Ricki, who turned towards the furious woman, the blood drained from his face. Crass held out her

golden hand, which twitched with mechanical malevolence as she brought it up towards Ricki's throat.

'Give the envelope to me now, boy, and I won't hurt you.'

Ricki's brow knotted into a frown, his nostrils flared and his cheeks flushed with anger. With incredible ferocity, he shouted, 'Never!'

Ricki struck out with his foot, slamming his toes into Crass' shin.

Ricki spotted Josh and Maddy hiding under the display case. He sprinted towards them and fell to the floor on his stomach. Josh and Maddy each grabbed a hand and yanked Ricki under the display case, just as a golden fist slammed into the ground inches from his trailing foot. The children shot to their feet on the other side and sprinted for the exit. A great commotion broke out as Crass clashed with the security guards, but the children didn't pause for a second. Sarah Van de Velde pleaded with them to stop, but Josh pushed the museum door open and they fled into the streets. Police sirens could be heard in the distance.

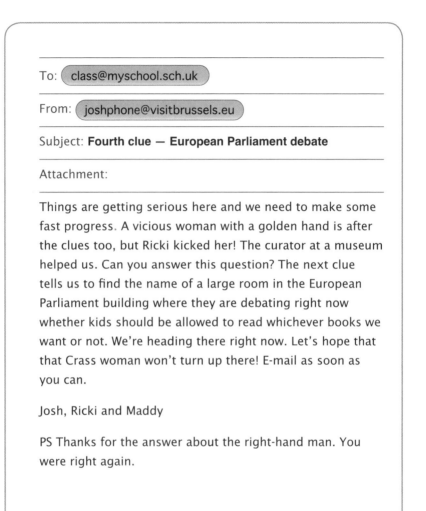

To: class@myschool.sch.uk

From: joshphone@visitbrussels.eu

Subject: **Fourth clue — European Parliament debate**

Attachment:

Things are getting serious here and we need to make some fast progress. A vicious woman with a golden hand is after the clues too, but Ricki kicked her! The curator at a museum helped us. Can you answer this question? The next clue tells us to find the name of a large room in the European Parliament building where they are debating right now whether kids should be allowed to read whichever books we want or not. We're heading there right now. Let's hope that that Crass woman won't turn up there! E-mail as soon as you can.

Josh, Ricki and Maddy

PS Thanks for the answer about the right-hand man. You were right again.

Chapter 7

CLEAR AS MUD

'We have to go to the police, Ricki,' said Josh, 'That woman was crazy. We don't know what we're mixed up in. Why did she want the clues so badly?'

'It's obvious. She's after the crown too,' Ricki replied. Josh sighed, unable to think of a better explanation himself. Ricki was looking around. 'So this is the plenary chamber. The plenum itself.'

The three children were looking down from the visitor's gallery into a large semicircular room filled with rows and rows of chairs facing a central platform, where a lively debate was in progress.

Having received an answer from school, the children had decided to take a tour of the European Parliament building for any further clues. Maddy, who had been listening to a handheld digital guide, turned to Josh.

'We must solve the last of my dad's clues,' she said emphatically. 'If we involve the police, they'll take the envelope away from us and we'll be left with nothing.'

'Maddy's right,' replied Ricki. 'We've only got one shot
at finding the treasure — and finding Maddy's dad, of course.
Besides, the police will have locked that crazy Crass woman up
in prison.'

'I think we should keep out of sight,' said Maddy. 'This
place is too public.'

'You've got a point,' said Ricki. 'What do people do in here
anyway?'

'Weren't you listening in the visitor's centre?' said Josh.
'This is where the Members of the European Parliament meet

and debate. They sit in groups with other MEPs who share more or less the same ideas. Then they debate new laws and how much money the EU can spend. If you'd bothered listening, some of them speak English, they've been debating whether books should have age restrictions, like films and video games. They've been fighting it out down there and what they decide will affect us directly.'

'As long as I can still read Tintin, I'll be happy. What are those rooms over there?' asked Ricki, pointing at some glazed walls.

'Everyone speaks in their own language. Those are booths where the interpreters sit. With these headphones here you can listen to all MEPs in English, even if they speak Greek,' Josh replied.

'If you two are quite done with the tour, let's go,' said Maddy decisively.

'Before we do, where can I buy a bottle of water? I'm parched,' said Ricki.

'Can't you just get some tap water?' asked Maddy irritably.

'But I was told you can't drink from the taps on the continent,' replied Ricki.

'Wow, you are behind the times,' scolded Maddy. 'It's perfectly safe because of the strict laws they made right here in the European Parliament.'

Several minutes later, the three children were sitting on a secluded bench in Leopold Park behind the European Parliament. Maddy was holding a clue from the envelope unfolded on her lap.

Ricki spotted an instruction on the sheet: 'Filter out the four-letter words'.

'I think it means that there are hidden words in these sentences here,' said Josh, pointing at a column of sentences.

'I'm so sorry,' said Maddy suddenly. Josh and Ricki stared at her in surprise. 'I thought this was just one of my dad's challenges, but this is really serious. I should have told you before. I don't know very much about his job, but he works for a secret government agency fighting organised crime. What I do know is that my dad must be in trouble and he's relying on me to solve these clues.'

To: class@myschool.sch.uk

From: joshphone@visitbrussels.eu

Subject: **Fifth clue — Filter out the four-letter words**

Attachment: waterfilter.doc

New clue, guys! Can you give us a hand? We've come across a document about cleaning water. Can you find out some more about cleaning and testing drinking water? What do you know about filtering? We think there might be some four-letter words hidden in the sentences on the attached sheet, but we're struggling to 'filter' them out. Any help appreciated,

Josh, Ricki and Maddy

CHAPTER 8

BREAKING NEWS

The three children were sitting on the bench studying the phone screen.

'That's a strange word,' muttered Josh. 'I hope they've got it right.'

'Yes, they have,' she said enthusiastically. 'I know the place. The clue word is the name of another EU building: the Justus Lipsius building. It's right opposite the European Commission offices with all those flags. It's only a few hundred metres from here.'

They headed north out of the park on to a nearby street. As they turned into the next street, Maddy stopped dead in her tracks. The boys turned to see her staring through the window of a bar. A news channel was visible on a wall-mounted television. There was no mistaking the scene live on screen: policemen were cordoning off Sarah Van de Velde's museum with blue and white tape; two paramedics were loading a stretcher into the back of an ambulance, which then tore off, lights whirling. A news ticker of bold text scrolled across the bottom of the screen:

MYSTERIOUS ATTACK ON MISSING CHILDREN — SECURITY GUARD INJURED – DANGEROUS FEMALE SUSPECT ESCAPED

The three of them quietly opened the bar door and stepped inside, transfixed by the sights on the TV screen. Suddenly, a familiar face appeared on the screen: Sarah Van de Velde. The children strained to hear what she was saying. She said something in French and then swapped to English:

'Children, if you see this, please contact me or the police immediately. The emergency number is 112 in Europe. We can help you. Call us please.'

Maddy said aloud what they were all thinking, 'Suspect escaped. We need to move fast.'

'No, Maddy,' said Josh. 'With Crass on the loose we have no choice now. We've got to contact the police.'

Ricki interrupted immediately, 'No way!' he said. 'You do what you like, I'm going with Maddy.' He stood next to her, crossing his arms, daring his friend to disagree. For good measure, Ricki added, 'And, what's more, you owe her for ripping apart her favourite bear back at the market!'

'Ashes to ashes, fluff to fluff,' he intoned solemnly, hanging his head.

Josh knew he was beaten. Shaking his head he said, 'Let's have a look at the next clue then.

Maddy gave Ricki a sly wink.

With that, they quickly bought some woolly hats and scarves to better disguise themselves and slipped into the backstreets of Brussels.

To: class@myschool.sch.uk

From: joshphone@visitbrussels.eu

Subject: **Sixth clue — Toy safety**

Attachment: missingletters.doc 📎

URGENT. Thanks for the answer to the last clue. We've figured out that it relates to another famous EU building here in Brussels. Now, this next clue's a bit weird. We think we need to have a closer look at some cuddly toys! Can you do the same? We're heading for a toy shop now. Please get back to us as soon as you can.

J., R. and M.

Chapter 9

THE CHARADE

It was nearly dusk and small, motionless clouds were beginning to glow pink above the rooftops. The three children were discussing the e-mail they had just received.

'So, how come your bear didn't have a label with a CE mark on it?' asked Josh.

'I'm not sure. It was very old I guess, before the EU brought in the safety rules,' replied Maddy.

'Is that it? Is that all that's left?' Ricki asked frowning.

Having left the toy shop, they were sifting through the envelope of clues. 'Yes,' replied Maddy, 'there's just this one sheet.'

Ricki let out a growl of frustration. 'But none of it makes sense. We've got all the words now, but they're meaningless. The only link between them is the European Union, and now all we've got is this.'

Ricki jabbed his finger down accusingly on a piece of paper covered in rows and columns of letters set inside a circle. The two others looked down. They all scoured the jumble of letters for some sort of meaning.

'Hang on, look,' exclaimed Josh. 'There's a word hidden there. It's just a simple word search!'

'What word, where?' demanded Maddy.

'Here. Atomium,' he pointed excitedly. 'Quick, look for other words.'

'There's a column of letters missing,' said Ricki, his eyes bright with concentration.

'You know what this is?' said Maddy. 'It's called a charade. It's one of my dad's favourite puzzles. A charade is the full clue. It's made up of words from separate clues, which must be all the other clue words we've found!'

'I'll e-mail it to our school,' said Josh pulling out his smartphone. 'I think you're right, Maddy. And if Ricki is correct, it'll lead us to the centre of the EU.'

To: (class@myschool.sch.uk)

From: (joshphone@visitbrussels.eu)

Subject: **The final clue — Charade sheet**

Attachment: charade.doc 📎

This is it, the last clue. We think it's some sort of word search. Maybe you use the other clue words to find the word. We're hoping it will reveal where we can find Maddy's dad (or the crown!). Maybe you could search on a map or a satellite image. It's urgent. We're running out of time.

Thanks,

J., R. and M.

Chapter 10

THE ROUNDABOUT SHOWDOWN

It was getting dark and the temperature was dropping rapidly. Nearby, Josh was peering down at the screen of his smartphone.

'Come on,' Josh urged impatiently, 'why haven't they replied yet?'

'Give it a few more minutes, Josh,' said Maddy. 'Your friends at school have come through for us before. Try refreshing your e-mails. There, you've got a message.'

'That's it! Of course, it's a roundabout!' exclaimed Josh a few seconds later. 'Thank you, school! They've sent a map too. And just as we thought, the roundabout is at the heart of the EU quarter. Look, it's next to the Berlaymont and Justus Lipsius buildings!'

'What's up?' Ricki asked, holding up a large plastic bag.

'We've been sent the answer to the charade, so if you're done with your retail therapy, can we get going? What on earth have you been buying anyway?' asked Josh.

Ricki tapped the side of his nose twice. 'Treasure hunting tools, me hearties,' he replied with a wink.

An hour later, the three children were sitting on a bench in the middle of the Schuman roundabout. 'This is so frustrating!' Ricki said between clenched teeth. 'The crown's right here. It's so obvious. It's right under our noses, but with all these people around we can't get at it.'

With Ricki's words in mind, they all stared at the surrounding pavement and at the twelve flowerbeds set within it. The instant they had arrived, they had made the connection. Twelve missing golden stars. Twelve muddy, overgrown flowerbeds. Surely that wasn't a coincidence?

'Why did your dad choose such a public place, Maddy?' demanded Josh.

'I don't know,' she replied casting her eyes downwards. Josh felt a pang of guilt; there was no sign of her dad anywhere.

Ricki was fumbling to assemble some strange instrument. Consulting some instructions, he breathed a sigh of relief and said, 'Right, this last bit clips on to … there. Done! Let's see if it works. Hold up something metal for me.'

Josh pulled a handful of euros out of his pocket and held them out bunched in his fist. Ricki raised the end of his newly assembled metal detector and held it several inches above Josh's outstretched hand.

All of a sudden, a high-pitched buzz sounded. Ricki made some final adjustments, until he was satisfied that it was detecting the metal clearly and accurately.

'I've got to admit, buying the detector at the toy shop was a great idea,' said Josh.

'Yeah, and don't forget these,' said Ricki beaming. He reached into the toy shop bag and pulled out three short-handled spades. 'Ready to dig, maties!'

The children had waited patiently for another hour. The cold of the night was seeping into their bones. Eventually, the last few passers-by had made their way home. The children rose and walked to the nearest flower bed. Ricki switched on the metal detector and began to sweep it carefully back and forth over the dark soil and grass. Almost immediately, a high-pitched buzz startled the children and Ricki quickly withdrew the detector for fear of attracting attention.

'No way,' muttered Josh. 'It can't be that easy.'

'Dig,' said Maddy.

It was Josh who unearthed the first one. Lifting away a slab of grass, he saw it poking out of the moist soil: a five-pointed star made of solid gold. Maddy knelt down and pulled

it gently from the ground, an orange glint reflected in her wide eyes. 'Dad,' she whispered, stuffing the precious star into her bag.

As predicted, each of the 12 flowerbeds contained one of the stars that were easily found using Ricki's detector. In one flowerbed, they discovered the golden headband too. Before long, Maddy was placing the final star safely into her bag.

It was at that precise moment that all hell broke loose. Without warning, a dark figure emerged from behind a hedge at the edge of the roundabout and rushed towards them. The children recognised the tall figure and the deep, callous voice immediately.

'Bring that crown to me now,' barked Crass. Maddy stared back at her defiantly and gripped the bag tightly to her chest.

'No,' Maddy's reply was soft but determined. 'It's not yours. It should be in a museum. It belongs to the citizens of Europe.'

'That's enough, girl,' snapped Crass. 'That crown is rightfully mine. I am the direct descendent of the noble Marcus Licinius Crassus. Through me, his great name lives on!'

'Rubbish!' retorted Maddy fiercely. 'My dad told me about people like you. You're just a common thief buying and selling on the black market. My dad's spent his life rescuing stolen artworks from greedy people like you.'

'So it was your dad who broke into my villa and sent us all on this treasure hunt? Well, his plan seems to have failed. Where is he now?' Crass sneered.

'I'll find him somehow,' Maddy responded defiantly.

'Oh, I doubt that,' Crass replied. 'I followed him to the flea market, but he must have known I was onto him and he escaped in the mist. But don't worry, I've sent some friends to track him down and my friends don't play nice. Now give me the crown.'

With a growl of anger, Crass approached Maddy decisively, her golden claw snapping open and shut in front of her.

'Back off, Crass!' shouted Josh, trying to hide his terror. He swung his spade as hard as he could into her stomach. Crass doubled over winded, an oomph of air escaping her lungs. But she was not to be denied and quickly regained her footing and stepped closer to Maddy.

'Oi, did you miss me?' shouted Ricki, waving his metal detector. Crass stopped and turned to face him.

'You! You won't escape me this time,' she snarled and began to step towards Ricki. Whilst his plan to draw Crass away from Maddy had worked, Ricki hadn't really thought through what he would do next. With Crass no more than 6 feet away, he lifted the metal detector up like a weapon to defend himself from Crass's hideous metal pincers. Ricki watched, the detector held only inches from her claw, as the metal hand began to twitch and jerk uncontrollably. Crass let out a shriek of pain. Alert to what was happening, Josh shouted, 'It's the detector, the magnetic field must be interfering with the electronics in her hand!'

Ricki jabbed the detector forward to make contact with Crass's hand. It spasmed violently and rapidly and Crass's face contorted. Josh was suddenly aware of the roar of revving engines, the screech of tyres under heavy braking and commands being shouted by onrushing uniformed men. Blue lights swept across the scene. Sirens wailed. A familiar voice rang out: 'Children, run to me now!'

It was Sarah Van de Velde, her arms outstretched towards them. Josh didn't hesitate, sprinting the short distance across the pavement and into her embrace. Ricki waited only a few seconds longer, allowing time for the approaching police officers to reach Crass and tackle her to the ground.

'Thank you, oh thank you,' said Ricki breathlessly, hugging Sarah closely. 'How did you know where we were?'

'A lucky guess,' she replied soothingly. 'I told the police there was a connection to Schuman. We tried Schuman station, the metro and then here.'

'Sarah, we did it,' said Josh. 'We found the treasure. The cursed crown. It's not in one piece, but we found it all.' Sarah looked baffled.

Ricki jumped in, 'Crass was after the crown too, see? Oh, it's easier to show you. Maddy's got the pieces in her bag.'

They all looked up. Maddy was standing proudly holding up her bag. Sarah rushed over to hug her.

'Oh, you brilliant girl,' she said softly as Maddy melted into her warm embrace.

☆ ☆ ☆

TWO MONTHS LATER

It was a baking summer's day in the capital of Italy, Rome. Josh and Ricki were thankful to be inside, enjoying the relative coolness of the Palazzo dei Conservatori museum.

The boys stood side by side nervously, in front of a large audience gathered to celebrate the unveiling of the museum's latest exhibit: the cursed crown of Crassus. On a tall plinth, the marble bust of Crassus stared haughtily out over the group. On top of the statue, gleaming with polished brilliance, sat the restored crown of twelve golden stars.

The crowd fell silent as the director of the museum stood to introduce the President of the European Commission.

'Ladies and gentlemen,' the president began. 'It is my honour to open this new exhibit today. The Corona Crassus is a truly remarkable artefact and an invaluable piece of European heritage. However, it gives me even more pleasure to introduce you to these five remarkable people, without whom this wonderful treasure would still be lost. These three children have shown incredible bravery, resourcefulness and honesty, and we thank them with all our hearts.'

The crowd clapped loudly. Ricki and Josh smiled at each other awkwardly and then both looked over to where Maddy was standing between a woman and a man. Maddy was beaming.

'In addition, I must pay tribute to Sarah Van de Velde for her courage and determination,' continued the president. Maddy smiled up at Sarah next to her and gave her a quick hug.

'Finally, we owe a huge debt to this gentleman,' said the president, indicating the handsome, dark-haired man on the other side of Maddy. 'This is Maddy's dad. He will tell you that he was just doing his job, but as you can see his job involves dangers we can only imagine.'

All eyes turned to Maddy's dad. His right arm was still in plaster and held in a sling, but his face was no longer bruised from when Crass's thugs had caught up with him.

The president concluded his speech, 'This gentleman was genuinely lucky to escape with his life and we must remember that his bravery, intelligence and integrity are vital in the daily fight against organised crime and art theft.'

The museum erupted with applause again. Maddy's dad gave the audience a polite nod of appreciation. Maddy looked up at him proudly and slipped her arm through his.